Gorp's Secret

An Empowering Tale in Pumpernickel Park

Body Privacy . . . Every Child's Right!

Story by Gorp as told to Sherri Chessen

Illustrated by Linda Bronson

The Gorp Group, LLC

Library of Congress Control Number: 2008920974

Summary: A poem teaching children about child abuse and body privacy

ISBN: 978-0-9724249-3-6

Project Management by BookStudio, LLC, Encinitas, California, www.bookstudiobooks.com
Design and Layout by Monika Stout, Zuppa Design, Encinitas, California

Published by The Gorp Group, LLC

1-888-729-4677 (PAX-GORP)

Printed in Hong Kong

I wish I may,
I wish I might,
keep the children
safe tonight.

I wish I might,
I wish I may,
keep the children
safe all day.

The wish behind
this little rhyme
is to keep you safe
ALL the time!

This book is
dedicated to YOU
with love
from,
Gorp

I'd rather be talking of happy things
like flying kites and soaring swings.
But to keep you safe
you have to know
when touching's wrong
and you must say "NO!"

I wish that I could change things,
I wish I had a tool
to make the world just perfect
and people never cruel.

But that is not reality,
so listen hard and well.
Just know that Gorp's sad secret
is difficult to tell.

Bright and early Monday morning,
and time to go to school.
Muffin kids and Cupcakes
walk together as a rule.

One little Muffin miss
was feeling kind of crumby,
her head so low,
that down below,
tears dripped right on her tummy.

The other Muffin cousins,
and the Cupcake kids as well,
kept asking why she felt so sad.
Missy Muffin wouldn't tell.

When they got to school that day
the muffin felt much worse,
and asked her teacher, Ms. Meringue,
if she could see the nurse.

Missy went to nurse's room,
which was sunshiny and bright.
The Muffin just began to cry.
Her words were stuck real tight.

The nurse was oh so thoughtful
and for the Muffin's sake,
just let her lie real quiet.
Nurse was an Angel Cake!

Angel Cake was a school nurse,
but she also was a mother,
and Muffin's silent, teary way
brought memories of another.

That memory was a little boy,
Pumpkin Pie who had no Pa.
He was always bright and bubbly,
then his mother married . . . the Claw!

The Bear Claw seemed a nice man
who made a ton of money.
He bought the Pie Kids lots of stuff,
and called his new wife, "Honey!"

They all appeared so happy,
they loved to be together,
except the little Pumpkin boy
who was underneath the weather!

He always had a tummy ache
'n' wouldn't look you in the eye.
His teacher mentioned it to nurse
who thought at least she'd try . . .

. . . to start a conversation
with the former friendly boy,
to see if he would tell her
what was shmooshing all his joy!

At first the boy was silent,
like he was scared to tell,
and then the secrets tumbled out
with lots of tears as well.

He told of Bear Claw Daddy
coming to his bed at night
and touching him all over.
Pie felt it wasn't right.

Was he at fault?
Was Pie to blame?
Did he do something wrong?
Pie started to cry,
he didn't know why,
but these feelings just didn't belong.

Then one day
Pie saw a play
and things began to click.
It said we must hear,
and hear it real clear,

It's the TOUCHERS who are sick!

NO TOUCHING BY OTHERS.....

In the play they told him
private parts are his alone,
and others shouldn't touch them,
even folks at home!

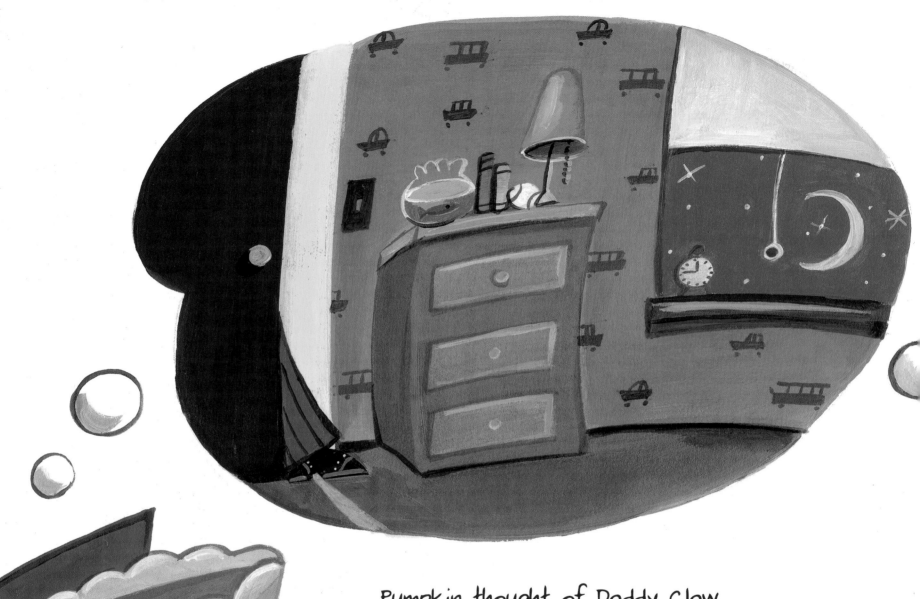

Pumpkin thought of Daddy Claw
and how he'd let Pie know
that he was the pet,
Daddy's favorite, yet
what a strange way to show . . .

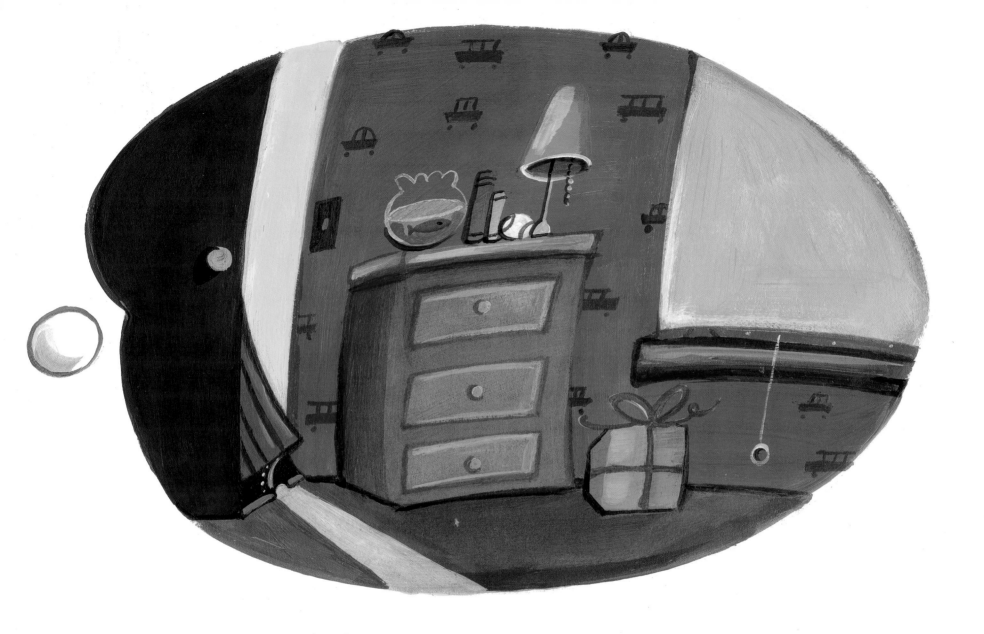

. . . that Pumpkin was the one he loved.
It didn't seem quite right
that he crept to Pie's room
by the light of the moon
after everyone else said good night.

In the play they also said
that's not how it should be.
But don't run and hide,
Mr. Claw's sick inside.
The blame is on HIM, don't you see?

Pumpkin heard the message.
"It's the TOUCHER who's not well.
If someone tries to touch you,
scream 'NO' . . . then TELL, TELL, TELL!"

Pie tried to tell his mother,
but she wouldn't hear a word.
She said, "The Claw is perfect,
your story is absurd."

But Pumpkin wasn't giving up.
He was feeling really strong.
He'd go on the double
and not get in trouble,
'cuz it wasn't he who was wrong!

Pie knew he's the boss of his body.
Pie knew he's in charge of it all.
He knew he was right,
and was loving his might.
He felt he was 90 feet tall!

So Pumpkin told his teacher
and she helped the little boy
by getting care
for everyone there,
giving Pumpkin back his joy!

25

The muffin girl sat up then,
tears running from her eyes.
"I need to tell my secret.
I feel I'm holding lies!

"I've been afraid for weeks now
when Napoleon comes to sit.
He's only fourteen,
but he can be mean.
He touches and even will hit!"

Nurse listened hard to Missy
and believed each word that came.
Some other kids had told as well,
their stories much the same.

Angel Cake would help the kids.
Telling starts the ball.
Adults have to be told,
you have to be bold,
then they can help us all!

"Worry no more," said Angel Nurse
"And dry those big, brown eyes.
Your secret's out
so smile and shout.
Telling really is wise!"

Missy hugged the Angel Nurse,
said thanks with all her heart.
For a little soul, just six years old,
this was a bright, new start!

MY PROMISE TO GORP

Because of Missy Muffin
And the boy called Pumpkin Pie,
I know for sure my body
is for me, myself, and I!

If someone tries to touch me,
please understand this well,
I won't stay quiet!
I'll start a riot!
And tell, and tell, and TELL!

Gorp's secret has empowered me,
and now I feel just right.
No touching by others
what my bathing suit covers,
and I'll say it with all of my might:

NO TOUCHING BY OTHERS
WHAT MY BATHING SUIT COVERS!!

NO TOUCHING BY OTHERS
WHAT MY BATHING SUIT COVERS!!!

X
_____
Please sign here if you agree with Gorp's Promise

. . . and you'll live happier ever after.

Because of the dire, delicate subject matter,
Gorp and I went kicking and screaming into this project.
Thank you for the gentle (but very effective) pushing from
Martha Burke of The Advocates in Hailey, Idaho, Rochelle Modean,
a Child Protection Activist, and Suzanne Lannon of First Witness in Duluth,
Minnesota, and Dr. Wilene Lampert of the Southern Arizona Children's Advocacy Center
in Tucson. We couldn't have (wouldn't have) done this book without you.

Big hugs to the best focus group ever: Maya Chessen, Charlotte Lehmann,
Anna and Lily Cork, Calder and Anik Zarkos, Jessica Dean and Stephanie Crain.
I know you'll recognize your input. It was vital!

The collective encouragement for this book has been mind-boggling, and my family and friends
are no exception . . . just exceptional! Special thanks for their tireless support to my children,
to my brother, Peter Chessen, and to Lucy Wilson and Donna Lorix, Gorp's "other moms."
And a huge hug of gratitude to Griffith Printing in St. Paul, MN.

A plethora of thanks to Mary Lewis Grow and the Student Pledge Against Gun Violence.
Gorp is very proud to be a part of this ongoing, brilliant effort.

Without the loving expertise and awesome guidance of Karla Olson of BookStudio
and Pam Swartz of Cloud Nine Press, we'd still be on Square One.

Finally to my world-class friend, Bob Tauber, my anchor and
my wings . . . ..Gorp and I thank and love each of you!

33

Gorp was born to be a symbol of all things good and non-violent. He helps children learn lessons like respect and responsibility while being loving, kind, friendly, and fair. When Gorp isn't busy writing, helping others, or on the rainbow, he lives with Sherri Chessen, wherever she may be. Gorp loved when Sherri was a Romper Room teacher on TV, as she always saw him in the Magic Mirror.

Illustrator Linda Bronson has illustrated more than ten books for children, including The Three Funny Friends by Charlotte Zolotow and Moe McTooth by Eileen Spinelli. She lives with her husband Charlie and daughter Frances in an old farmhouse in upstate Connecticut.

If you'd like to know more about Gorp,
please visit his website at:

WWW.THEGORP.COM

You can also call at 1-888-729-4677 (PAX-GORP)

He even has an Email address
gorp2@earthlink.net

Thank you for being strong, for
standing up for yourself, and
knowing when touching is NOT O.K.
BODY PRIVACY IS YOUR RIGHT!

We love you . . .